Coláiste Mhuire / MIE

R11467X2911

2nd
4.50

WHERE'S JACKO ?

my s

D1628141

my book

_____

Chimps – very easy books for beginners
Large type
Short words
Short sentences
An illustration on every page
And fun!
With a twist in the tale!

This is the sixth **Chimp**
The others are:
Cookie the Cat
Cookie and Curley
Flash Fox and Bono Bear
Two Mad Dogs
Back up the Beanstalk

Tony Hickey

Illustrated by Terry Myler

THE CHILDREN'S PRESS

To

Lucy and Leon Folan

First published 2004 by
The Children's Press
an imprint of Anvil Books
45 Palmerston Road, Dublin 6

2 4 6 8 7 5 3 1

© Text Tony Hickey 2004
© Illustrations Terry Myler 2004

All rights reserved. No part of this publication may
be reproduced, stored in a retrieval system, or
transmitted in any form or by any means, electronic,
mechanical, photocopying, recording or otherwise,
without the prior permission of the publishers.

ISBN 1 901737 47 0

Typeset by Computertype Limited
Printed by Colour Books Limited

Contents

1 Susie

Jacko was a chimp with soft brown fur and big round circles under his eyes.

He was Jason's very best friend. Anywhere Jason went, Jacko went too.

When Jason was a baby, Jacko would sit beside him in his push-car.

Every day Jason's mum would take him and Jacko to the shops with her.

They had a great time
looking at the people and the
cars and the shops.

Most of all, Jason loved the
dogs they met along the way.

But Jacko thought the cats
were the best.

'Look at how high they can
jump!' he would say.

When Jason was older, he took Jacko to the local play school with him.

All the other children there had toys.

There were lions and tigers and frogs and bears and cats and dogs.

But none of them was as nice or as cuddly as Jacko.

The little girl, who sat beside Jason, was so fond of him that she wanted to take him home.

One day when her mum called for her, she pointed to Jacko and said, 'I want Jacko.'

'But, Susie,' said her mum, 'you have loads and loads of toys at home.'

'I don't want any of them. I want Jacko.'

'But you can't have him. He belongs to Jason.'

'I'll give him my giraffe
instead. He's much bigger,' said
Susie. 'Or my tiger. But I must
have Jacko.'

Jason was afraid she was
going to grab Jacko. He held
the chimp so tightly that Jacko
felt squashed. He could hardly
breathe.

'Don't be silly, Susie,' said
her mum. 'I'll tell you what …
I'll get you another chimp, just
like Jacko.'

But Susie's new chimp
wasn't at all like Jacko.

He didn't have a big friendly smile. He looked cross and bad tempered.

Susie, who was a very spoilt little girl, threw the new chimp into a corner.

'I want Jacko,' she said.

The teacher, who had heard this, moved Jason to another group, in the hope that Susie would forget Jacko.

But Jason was still worried.

2 Jacko Disappears

A week later Mum, Jason and Jacko went to the mall.

Matty Head, the teen-age pop star, was coming there to launch his new record.

But Matty was late.

Because it was a very warm day, Mum took Jason into the café for a nice cool drink.

Susie and her mum were there as well.

Jason had just finished his drink when the crowd outside shouted, 'Matty is here!'

Everyone rushed out of the café. They all wanted to be at the front of the crowd.

A long, shiny, white car with dark windows stopped outside the record shop.

Everyone cheered as Matty got out and waved his guitar.

Then Jason remembered
Jacko. He tugged Mum's skirt.

'I've left Jacko in the café!'

They both ran back inside
but Jacko had vanished.

'Someone might have given
him to the girl at the counter,'
said Mum. 'We'll ask her.'

But the girl said, 'I'm sorry
but he wasn't handed in.'

Mum said, 'Maybe someone
who knew that Jacko was yours
took him for safe keeping.'

'The only people in the café
who knew that Jacko belonged
to me were Susie and her
mum,' said Jason.

'Then I'm sure that if they
have Jacko, they'll bring him
back to you,' said Mum.'

22

Jason spent the whole of the afternoon at the window, but they never came.

When he was going to bed, he had one last look.

That night there was a big
storm. The wind howled and
the rain poured down.

Jason lay in bed and hoped
Jacko was safe. Since he first
got him from his dad, they
had never been parted.

24

Next day it was bright and sunny again, so Mum and Jason went to Susie's house.

But Susie said she had seen nothing.

'I ran out of the café before you did. How could I have seen Jacko?'

Jason knew she was telling a lie. He had seen her still in the café when he had rushed out to see Matty Head.

Susie's mum couldn't have cared less about Jacko or whether he was lost or stolen.

'Maybe someone took him for a joke,' she yawned, 'then threw him away. He's only a toy.'

Jason and Mum went back to the shopping mall to see if they could find Jacko there.

There was no sign of him.

Then they went up and
down all the roads nearby.

They searched high. They
searched low.

They looked into front
gardens, along the gutters, even
under parked cars.

But Jacko had vanished into
thin air.

3 To the Rescue

In Susie's bedroom, which was at the front of the house, all her toys had heard what had been said at the hall door.

Well, I never,

'Well, I never,' said the giraffe, who had seen Jason and his mum walking sadly away from the house. 'Telling a lie like that when all the time she has Jacko hidden in the press.'

Teddy, who was a big happy bear, opened the door of the press and spoke to Jacko.

'Not to worry!' he said. 'We'll get you home somehow.'

Jacko just nodded his head. Two big tears rolled down his cheeks. He was too upset to speak.

He missed Jason. He missed his home. And he hated being locked up in a dark press.

'Now we have to think of a rescue plan,' said Teddy.

'We'll get Rusty, the dog next door, to help,' said the giraffe.

We'll get Rusty

He banged on the window with his head until Rusty came running up.

When he heard the whole story, he said, 'Of course I'll take Jacko home. Just lower him out of the window.'

Jacko was really afraid. He closed his eyes as the giraffe lowered him as far as he could out of the open window.

Then the giraffe let go of the chimp and Rusty caught him safely and gently in his mouth.

'Where to?' he asked as Jacko climbed on his back.

'Number 16, Larch Road,' said Jacko. He was so excited to be going home that he could hardly speak.

'Where's that?' asked Rusty.

'Turn right at the end of the road,' the giraffe called out. 'Then left, then right.'

'Good luck,' said all the
animals as Rusty set off with
Jacko on his back.

'They'll need more than luck
to find their way to Larch
Road,' growled the tiger. 'That
Rusty may be a nice guy but
he's as thick as a plank.'

4 The Tabby Cat

The tiger had Rusty taped.

When he and Jacko left the house, they turned right, then left. Then the dog stopped.

'Right or left?' he asked.

'Right,' said Jacko.

'Are you sure? I thought it was, *right-left-left*. Two lefts.'

'No, it was *right-left-right*.'

No, they said right.

'I'm sure there were *two* left turns. I said to myself at the time, "It's right to turn left." Ha! Ha! That's funny, isn't it?'

And he turned left.

Jacko shook his head. It wasn't Larch Road.

After that, Rusty galloped up and down dozens of roads.

Jacko began to feel sick from all the jolting that he got from sitting on Rusty's back.

At last they stopped. 'I don't know where we are,' said Rusty, 'I think we may be lost.'

I don't know where we are

'Then we had better go back to Susie's house and start all over again,' said Jacko.

They went up and down
more roads and, more by luck
than anything else, found their
way back to Susie's house.

The toys leaned out of the
window.

'What happened?' they called.

'We got lost,' panted Rusty.
'But I'm going to try again.'

'Waste of time,' said the tiger.

'It certainly is.' Lulu, the persian cat who lived at Susie's, strolled into the bedroom. 'All dogs are dopes. If you want something done, ask a cat.'

'Is that so?' snarled Rusty.

'Yes, it is,' said Lulu. 'Now what's the problem.'

'We want to get Jacko back
to Jason at number 16 Larch
Road,' said Raggy Anne.

'Leave everything to me,'
said Lulu. 'And remember, you
should always ask a cat.'

She was about to jump down
into the garden when suddenly
it began to rain.

She moved away from the window. 'I can't go out in the rain,' she said. 'My lovely fur would get soaked.

'Then Susie's mum wouldn't let me into the drawing room – I'd ruin the carpet.'

'Who's a sugar baby then?' a
voice from the window sill said.

There, looking in at Lulu
and the toys, was a tabby cat.

'Afraid of a little rain?' the
tabby asked. 'Well never
mind. You stay in the house
and I'll take Jacko home.'

'But do you know the way?' asked Jacko.

'I know all the roads around here,' said the tabby cat. 'I've often seen you and Jason looking out of your window so I know just where you live.'

'Yes, but where do *you* live?'
Lulu asked crossly. 'You haven't
even got a name or a home.'

'And what good is a name if
you are afraid of a little drop
of rain?' replied the tabby cat.

The toys were delighted at this reply. Lulu could be very bossy and spiteful, using her sharp claws to hurt them.

Now all she could do was toss her head and stalk out of the bedroom.

The tabby jumped down into the garden.

'Right,' she said to Jacko. 'Jump up on my back.'

So, for the second time that day, Jacko set off for home.

Riding on the tabby cat's back
was much more comfortable
than being on Rusty's back.

The cat easily jumped over
walls, landing ever so gently.

She slipped under hedges.

She always knew when it was safe to cross busy roads.

When they met dogs, Jacko used to get weak with fright, but the tabby just glared at them until they got out of her way. Then she stalked past.

When they paused for a rest Jacko said to her, 'You are a very brave cat. How is it you have no name? And no home?'

'I like to go where I please when I please,' said the cat. 'Though I would like a nice warm home. Winters are cruel.'

49

'You could always come and live with me and Jason,' said Jacko. 'I'm sure his mum and dad wouldn't mind. We could call you "Tabby".'

'That sounds like a very good idea,' said the cat. 'Hold on tight. We're almost there.'

5 A Surprise

While Tabby and Jacko were
on their journey, Jason's dad
came home. He had been away
at sea with his ship.

When he heard that Jacko
was missing he talked to Jason.

'Don't worry, son,' he said.
'As soon as I have a cup of
coffee we'll go and look for him
again. Better put on your
wellies. It looks like rain.'

But Dad and Jason could not find Jacko anywhere.

They searched skips and litter boxes and under the shrubs in the park.

They called to the houses near the shopping mall and asked the people living there if they had seen Jacko.

The answer was always 'No.'

Dad and Jason even went to the Garda Station.

The garda in charge tried to cheer up Jason. 'We'll treat it as a 'missing chimp' case,' he said. 'We'll ask every squad car to keep a look-out for Jacko.'

But Jason couldn't cheer up.
He was sure Susie had stolen
Jacko and was hiding him.

But how could he prove this?

He walked sadly home,
holding his dad's hand.

His mum knew by his face
that there was no good news.

'Take off your wellies,' she said, 'and leave them in the porch. Then come in and we'll decide what we should do.'

Jason pulled off his wellies. He was about to put them behind a flower-pot when he gave a gasp of amazement.

Jacko, a big smile on his face, was sitting behind one of the flower-pots.

'How *did* you get here?' Jason managed to say.

'Tabby helped to rescue me from Susie's house,' said Jacko.

'Who is Tabby?' asked Jason.

'She's outside on the wall,' said Jacko.

Jason looked out of the porch window and saw a thin tabby cat looking back at him.

She waved her tail as if saying, 'Hello!'

'I told her she could come and live with us,' said Jacko.

Jason's dad came out into
the porch. He was wondering
why Jason wasn't coming in.

When he saw Jacko, he gave
a whoop of delight.

Mum came running out of the sitting room to see what was going on. She was amazed to see Jacko home again.

'But where was he?' she asked. 'How did he get here?'

'The tabby cat brought him home,' said Jason. 'Can we keep her? Her name is Tabby.'

'Well, I suppose that's the least we can do as a reward for finding Jacko,' said Mum.

Dad nodded in agreement and so not only did Jacko come safely back home but Tabby, the stray found a home.

'No place like it,' she purred.

When Susie next saw Jason
with Jacko, she was amazed.

And Jason and Jacko
decided not to tell her how
Jacko had escaped from the
press in her bedroom.

Tony Hickey is one of Ireland's most popular children's writers.

For The Children's Press he has also written the *Granny* books – *Granny Learns to Fly, Granny and the American Witch, Granny Green: Flying Detective*; the *Flip 'n' Flop* series – *Flip 'n' Flop, Flip 'n' Flop in Kerry, Flip 'n' Flop and the Movies*. Other titles include tales of the *Matchless Mice*, and *The Black Dog*, an adventure story set in his native county of Kildare.

Terry Myler has illustrated all the **Chimp** books. In addition, she has illustrated all the **Elephant** series (books to read if you're slightly older).

If you want to learn to draw yourself, have a look at her book *Drawing Made Easy*